DODSWORTH IN NEW YORK

Written and illustrated by

TIM EGAN

HOUGHTON MIFFLIN HARCOURT
BOSTON   NEW YORK

To my favorite aunt, Lorrie,

and my favorite step-uncle, Don.

Copyright © 2007 by Tim Egan

All rights reserved. Originally published in hardcover in the United States
by Houghton Mifflin Books for Children, an imprint of
Houghton Mifflin Harcourt Publishing Company, 2007.

First Green Light Readers edition, 2016.

Green Light Readers and its logo are trademarks of Houghton Mifflin Harcourt
Publishing Company, registered in the United States and/or other jurisdictions.

For information about permission to reproduce selections from this book, write to
trade.permissions@hmhco.com or to Permissions, Houghton Mifflin Harcourt
Publishing Company, 3 Park Avenue, 19th Floor, New York, New York 10016.

www.hmhco.com

The text of this book is set in Cochin.
The illustrations are ink and watercolor on paper.

The Library of Congress has cataloged the hardcover edition as follows:
Egan, Tim.
Dodsworth in New York / written and illustrated by Tim Egan.
p. cm.
Summary: When Dodsworth sets out for adventure, including a stop in
New York City before going to Paris, London, and beyond, he does not expect
a crazy duck to stow away in his suitcase and lead him on a merry chase.
[1. Voyages and travels—Fiction. 2. New York (N.Y.)—Fiction.
3. Ducks—Fiction. 4. Adventure and adventurers—Fiction.] I. Title.
PZ7.E2815Dod 2007
[E]—dc22
2006034522

ISBN: 978-0-618-77708-2 hardcover
ISBN: 978-0-547-24831-8 paperback

Printed in China
SCP 15 14 13 12 11 10
4500591312

CONTENTS

CHAPTER ONE
BREAKFAST

Dodsworth wanted adventure.

He wanted to fly in a plane.

He wanted to sail on a ship.

He wanted to see the world.

But first, he wanted breakfast.

He went to his favorite place,

Hodges' Café.

He loved Hodges' pancakes.

Everybody did.

They were the best pancakes in

the world.

Dodsworth walked into the café.

It was very early, so there was

nobody around.

Nobody, that is, but Hodges' duck.

Hodges' duck was crazy.

"Mornin'," said Dodsworth.

The duck just stared at him.

"May I please have some pancakes?"
asked Dodsworth.

The duck turned and jumped onto
a stool.

The duck started singing,

"Fluffy pancakes in the air.

Pancakes, pancakes everywhere!"

"Oh no," said Dodsworth.

The duck flew behind the counter.

He started throwing pancakes at

Dodsworth.

Dodsworth tried to catch the pancakes.

He caught three out of seven.

Hodges ran out from the kitchen.

He grabbed the duck.

"Sorry about that, Dodsworth,"

he said. "You're here bright and early."

"Yep," said Dodsworth, "I'm going on

an adventure."

"Where to?" asked Hodges.

"New York. Paris. London. You name it," said Dodsworth.

"Sounds exciting," said Hodges.

The duck said nothing.

Dodsworth finished his breakfast.

He bid farewell to Hodges.

Hodges wished him well.

Dodsworth tipped his hat and

pedaled away.

CHAPTER TWO
THE TRAIN

Dodsworth arrived at the train station.

He bought a ticket to New York.

From there he would sail across the ocean.

He was very excited.

The train started chugging along,
over hills and under bridges,
through fields and forests.
It was the start of a grand adventure.

Two hours later, Dodsworth went to
open his trunk.

As he lifted the lid, the duck jumped out.

"Finally!" said the duck. "I could
hardly breathe!"

Dodsworth couldn't believe it.

"What are you doing here?!" he shouted.

"Looking for excitement," said the duck.

"Where are we going?" he asked.

Dodsworth was not happy.

"WE are not going anywhere!" he shouted.
"I'M going on an adventure! Alone!
YOU are going back on the next train!"
The duck just looked out the window.
"This is fun," he said.

Dodsworth went up to the conductor.

"Can you please stop this train?" he asked.

"Not until New York," said the conductor.

Dodsworth was very upset.

He marched back to his room.

The duck had taken all of Dodsworth's
clothes out of the trunk.
He was lying on them.
"This is the life," he said.
Dodsworth was very angry.

"Get off my clothes!" he shouted.
"Look at the mess you made!"
"Whoa," said the duck, "calm down
   there, partner."
"I will not calm down!" shouted
   Dodsworth. "And I am not your
   partner!"

CHAPTER THREE
NEW YORK CITY

The next morning, the train pulled into
New York City.

Dodsworth bought a ticket for the duck
to go home.

He turned to give the duck the ticket.

He saw the duck getting on the subway.

Again, Dodsworth was very mad.

"Fine!" he shouted. "Good luck to you!"

He started walking to the boatyard.

"Paris, here I come," he grumbled.

He walked for a mile, but then he
stopped.
He knew how worried Hodges must be.
He knew he had to find the duck.
"All I wanted was a simple little adven-
ture," he said.

He walked around New York City all day.

Across the Brooklyn Bridge.

Up to Yankee Stadium and down to
Wall Street.

There was no sign of the duck, but
Dodsworth was amazed at the giant
buildings.

He headed over to Washington Square.

There were a lot of ducks and they all

looked the same.

A lady was feeding them bread.

Only one duck was throwing bread

back at the lady.

"Aha!" shouted Dodsworth.

He chased the duck down to the Hudson
River, but the duck got away again.
Dodsworth sat and watched the boats for
a while.
He thought he saw the duck on one of
the boats.
"Why would a duck take a boat?" he
wondered.

The boat was going to the Statue of
Liberty.

Dodsworth took the next boat.

He arrived at the statue and climbed to
the top.

There was no sign of the duck anywhere.

There was, however, a great view of
the city.

That night, Dodsworth checked into a
hotel near Central Park.
He kept trying to call Hodges on
the phone.
Still no answer.
At one point, he thought he saw the duck
in the park.
It was too dark to tell for sure.

In the morning, he walked to a diner
across from the park.

He ordered pancakes.

They were not as good as Hodges'.

Not even close.

Dodsworth watched as the park came
to life.

A band started playing music.

Folks started flying a kite.

A magician began doing tricks.

"I shall now pull a rabbit from my hat,"
said the magician.

He pulled out the duck instead.

"Aha!" screamed Dodsworth.

The duck took off.

Dodsworth tried to catch the duck all day.

He chased him up to Park Avenue.

Even though he couldn't find the duck,

Dodsworth liked how fancy everyone

was dressed.

Later, he saw the duck go into the
Museum of Modern Art.

Dodsworth searched and searched, but
he couldn't find the duck anywhere in the
museum, either.

That evening, he spotted the duck
walking into Radio City Music Hall.
A movie was playing, so it was really
dark.
Since Dodsworth couldn't see the duck,
he decided to just enjoy the movie.

After a while, somebody started throwing
popcorn at the screen.

Dodsworth knew who the somebody was.

He stood up and saw the duck.

"Aha!" he shouted.

"Shhh!" shouted everybody else.

The duck ran out and jumped onto a bus.

Dodsworth jumped into a taxicab.

"Follow that duck!" he said.

The taxi followed the duck.

The bus went to Coney Island.

Dodsworth watched the duck get on the

Ferris wheel.

He waited until just the right second.

"Gotcha!" he said as he grabbed the duck.

"Hey," said the duck, "how's it going?"

CHAPTER FOUR
GOING HOME

Dodsworth brought the duck to the

train station.

"You should be ashamed," said Dodsworth.

"You worried Hodges. You worried me.

You could have been lost forever."

"Sorry," said the duck.

The duck lowered his head.

Dodsworth put his hand on the duck.

"Oh, it's all right," he said. "Don't be sad."

The duck started snoring.

He was sound asleep.

Dodsworth went to a phone booth.

He called Hodges again.

"Hello?" said Hodges.

He sounded sad.

"Hodges!" shouted Dodsworth.

"I've got the duck! He's with me!"

Hodges screamed.

"That crazy duck! I've been worried

sick!"

"Sorry he ruined your adventure," said
Hodges.

"Ruined it? He *was* the adventure,"
said Dodsworth.

They both laughed.

"We'll head home on the next train,"
said Dodsworth.

Dodsworth went back to the duck.
To his great dismay, the duck was
gone again.
Dodsworth looked out the window.
The duck was getting on a boat.

Dodsworth ran and jumped on the boat.

The boat started sailing away.

"Hurry!" said Dodsworth. "Let's swim

back to shore!"

"No can do," said the duck. "I can't

swim."

"What?!" shouted Dodsworth. "You're a duck!"

"Sorry," said the duck. "Never learned how to swim."

The city became farther and farther away.

Dodsworth saw that the boat was going to Paris.

He went to the phone and called
Hodges again.

"Uh, hey," he said. "Listen. Everything is
fine. The duck is still with me, but, well,
it might be a little longer than we
thought."